SHANNA'S Teacher SHOW

by **Jean Marzollo**
Illustrated by **Shane W. Evans**

JUMP AT THE SUN
HYPERION BOOKS FOR CHILDREN
New York

I'm a teacher.

Wonder how
I know?

I'll give you 5 clues on today's Shanna Show.

Clue 1: lots of books.
Come and read with me.

Clue **2**: music. Here's an instrument to play.
May you have the tambourine?
Yes, Ducky, dear, you may.

And now we find we have arrived at Clue Number 3.
We will learn the alphabet all the way from A to Z!

Clue 4: numbers.
Count your fingers up to 10,

then your toes up to 20.
When you're finished, start again!

Clue **5**: lots of crayons.
My favorite one is blue.